Trees for the Forest

*by
Patricia
Cast*

From both of us
-- love

Pat

Trees for the Forest

.

*A Collection
of Myths*

.

by Patricia Cast

**Illustrated by
Rondi Anderson**

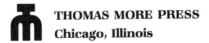

THOMAS MORE PRESS
Chicago, Illinois

ISBN 0—88347—096—9

Contents

THE
VISION
OF
RA

RA SAT, mighty and still, his great figure one with the throne that held him, both carved from a single block of stone. No dust fell on him in the sealed magnificence surrounding him, for no air moved. No light reached him. In majestic beauty he sat unseen while long centuries went by in silence. In the remote darkness which shielded his mystery he remained, unloved and still, while those men who knew or sensed his presence trembled in distant reverence. And Ra was content.

Then something made contact with Ra and his eternity was troubled into time. An awareness gradually moved through him that something was touching him. He felt a motion and did not know what it was, a strange and gentler sensation that suddenly reached a life he did not know he had and made him yearn to know. There came a rending which tore his stone and he felt himself broken. The unseen world moved round him and all was fear.

It was in his fear that consciousness returned. He felt his spirit in the stone, and

his spirit became aware. In fear he knew that he was no longer whole; in fear too he knew that his darkness was no longer familiar. Things had changed their positions and so had he. The sense of objects in particular places was gone and he no longer knew what surrounded him or where he was. The darkness of his majesty and awe had changed. It did not feel the same. As he grew more aware, he experienced again the strange, gentle sensation he had felt before. Slowly fear disappeared in yearning, and the god within him knew it was for light. Ra longed to see, believing that he once had seen, but his spirit could not yet prevail against the stone. He bent his strength to effort and became conscious of the changing heat and coolness of days in the one long single act of his will. Fear was forgotten.

It was remembered again when slowly light came to the spirit of Ra. He saw himself lying on the granite floor, torn from the throne which stood empty behind him. His feet were gone; they had remained attached to the pedestal, and the symbols of his glory were scattered around him. The shrine was broken and its treasures in disarray. Ra lay helpless, exposed to light and winds and heat. But light was glorious, glory beyond the sheath of gold that covered him partly still, and for all its strangeness seemed strangely old as if it were a place where he had dwelt in some forgotten age. Fear could not remain for long in light. Nor could content. He could not see himself and his broken parts upon the floor and be content. He felt the desire to rise up whole and stand; to stand—not even to sit upon the throne that remained in the shade of his temple—but to stand upright in the light. It was a far greater effort now, and an anguish he had never known. Not only to be whole in his mighty image, but even to be free of the stone itself and stand. He learned minutes as well as days in this pain as his spirit strained unyielding against the stone he could not shatter.

Workmen came to repair the desecrated and pillaged shrine, to restore to their god his proper majesty. They worked in awe of him, with eyes averted from his frightening humiliation. Furnishings were replaced and walls repaired, but the central shrine had to be rebuilt entirely. What remained of the old was pulled down. He was dragged away to be reunited to himself and then restored with due ceremony to his former place. A light shelter was built for him on holy ground to protect his sacredness.

Ra knew he had been moved. The sight of the order in which he had respectfully been placed increased his helplessness and increased his desire to stand free of the stone. More constant light reached him through the delicate linens of his tent and made him long for something not remembered.

It was a strange accident. An animal brushed by him. Ra had seen it come, he felt it, and heard the sounds it made. He knew the difference now between animals and men. In the secrecy of his shrine there had been nothing that lived, but since then he had learned that animals would touch him, they would look at him; men never did. Their eyes were lowered, and even in moving him, no one had dared to touch him with his hand. He had never seen a human face.

Now an animal brushed by him and did not pass on. It remained. He heard a voice. It was shaking and the calls were repeated again and again. The animal still remained. The voice calling and the touch of the animal both continued for some time and then there was silence.

The light suddenly increased as the tent curtains were drawn back, and a boy was in the opening, his face turning from one corner of the tent to another. The boy's eyes fixed upon the dog which was beside the head of Ra. There was a long pause while the boy stood motionless. Finally he advanced over the sand. Twice more he paused, then ran towards the stone figure and reached down to take the dog. As he did so, he looked full into the great face of Ra. He stopped still, the dog in his arms, and gazed long and steadily.

Ra felt something move as the boy gazed. It seemed as if he were in the eyes that looked at him. Suddenly the boy dropped his head, but Ra could still see his face. He got to his feet and ran from the tent and Ra went with him, still in the eyes of the boy, still seeing his face.

How long a time it was, he never knew. It could not have been many months, but in that time Ra no longer desired to stand. His spirit moved with the boy. He knew what it was to sit when the boy sat, to stand when the boy stood, to leap and run. He began to know other things: what it was to laugh and to weep. What the boy did he knew, he lived, and when the boy fell silent with a smile upon his lips Ra knew more, for he knew that the image of his face was imprinted deep in the boy's thought. There was a light on the boy's face at such times, surpassing the light that had once been so greatly desired. For the first time the sun god saw his own splendor and knew his power and beauty. He knew not only the boy's life, but his own. It was no longer through the boy's eyes that he looked when he saw him turn to another face, and saw the same light reflected, caught, and begin to grow. In the one spreading glory shared, Ra at last knew what he was.

It ended as suddenly as it began, with another animal, this time a snake. Ra underwent the pain and heartbreak of the boy's long hour of suffering, but glad to undergo it—even knowing what the end would mean.

As the boy died, his face faded from Ra's sight. Gradually sounds came to him of singing and of trumpets. Grey figures took shape and turned to brilliant colors, twisting and swaying, the backs of dancers going before him. He was surrounded by men bowing low. Once again he was seated on his throne, his great stone bulk towering high above the sweating bodies straining to draw his chariot. He was returning to his shrine. Flowers were scattered around him, crushed beneath the feet of his servants, and the scent reached him mingling with burning perfumes. Cymbals clashed. Gold glittered bright in the sunlight. Thousands accompanied him. But nowhere did Ra see a face, and nowhere did he see the light that was himself.

No longer content, but with the great patience of the gods, Ra suffered himself to be drawn through the tumultuous crowds and sealed once more in the magnificent tomb of his immortality.

SEVEN
TIMES
ROUND

IMJI shied across the road at the sudden cry from the trees. His companion, much younger, was close to him, sweating, ears pricked forward.

"What was it? Can it reach us?"

Imji regathered his lost control. "No," he said. "It can't touch us. We are on the road."

"Of course," said the other, believing, but not truly reassured, and—like Imji—still afraid.

The two of them were on a broad, straight road that looked white in the starlight and whiter still in contrast to the heavy growth of bush and trees that marched on each side of it. A low white parapet constituted the only barrier against the dark menace from which the strange cry had come. It took confidence to believe that it was sufficient protection. Imji could leap it himself in a moment.

"We are on the road," he repeated. "It is safe on the road."

How many times he had said that to himself, and to others; and perhaps he did not quite believe it. How could he still be

afraid? The road stretched ahead through the darkness, white and straight and familiar. Familiar; not because he had travelled it before, but because he had travelled so many just the same. He knew it was always safe, and yet he was afraid. His companion, journeying for the first time, had an excuse for terror, but Imji had not and wondered why he still feared.

Perhaps it was those strange memories that were not quite memories at all. He could not remember a particular time not connected with the roads, but there had been a time—or a ghost of a time—of watchfulness, of sudden flights, and pursuit, a vague sense of unknown fear waiting. It was long forgotten—if it had ever been. He did not remember it, but that same time was in the trees on each side of the road.

However, they were on the road, not in the trees. And the parapet that anyone could leap was a barrier never crossed within his memory. Imji was safe and rebuked himself for the movement of fear that had unnerved his young companion.

"When shall we reach it?" said the youngster.

"I do not know," said Imji. "These roads look all the same, but they are not the same in length. Some are long and some are short."

"Shall we find water along the way?" asked the anxious youngling.

"We always find water," replied Imji.

Before the sun had risen high the next day, they came to the end of the journey. To Imji there was nothing he had not seen before. The same white circle with the low parapet except where the different roads led away, towards the sun, the moon, the stars, or away from them. There was the same high wall at one point, intriguing, mysterious, and impenetrable. Also there was the same one to be sought: the elder, the one who ordered this small realm.

Pausing to look over the assembled group within the circle, Imji's experienced eye soon perceived him. Nudging his companion, Imji led the way.

This one was not so old; seasoned—yes,

but vigorous. Imji made a full courtesy, and reading the look quickly shot at him, the youngster did the same. The elder made no movement, gravely regarding them in silence. Imji spoke.

"We come in peace, and seek to be received among you."

Silence still; and still the elder regarded them. Finally he lowered his head in solemn politeness and moved towards them.

"Welcome, strangers! Enter the circle."

In not many days, they were no longer strangers. Imji no longer saw much of his companion of the road who had found younger and more congenial friends. He himself mingled well and easily among them all, for he was still in his prime, with muscles and nerves that served him instantly and well. He was valued by the circle and came to be valued by the elder for his combination of strength and experience. There were few with whom the elder could speak freely, but he began to speak with Imji. Eventually Imji ventured to ask what had been in his mind when he waited so long before admitting the two new strangers to the circle.

"Many things," said the elder. "You both were strong and we needed strength, but I feared that perhaps you were too strong and too wise—for there can be but one leader."

"My wisdom is great enough to know that," said Imji. "Did you think I wished to challenge you?"

"No," replied the other. "I read that in your eyes. You will challenge no one. You will not follow; but you will never lead."

Startled, Imji's horned head came up. "You say strange things."

"Perhaps. We shall see," smiled the elder.

After a moment's silence, Imji continued. "Was there more than that?"

"Yes," replied the elder. "I had to consider whether we were too many. We needed strength, but the circle has just so much. Last year, a large group came from the north. We could not have fed so many, so we had to fight them off."

"Fight them off!" cried Imji, "But were they not our kind?"

"Indeed they were; but what is that if we all die? There can be a certain number within the circle. When we are too few, we need more, and welcome strength. When there are too many, we must protect ourselves from those outside."

"So even we can be 'those outside' ! "

"Did you not know? I thought you wise," said the elder and moved away.

Imji stood for a long time, staring out at the trees with the words fixed in his brain.

Time went by, and the group seemed complete. Some died, and some few new strangers came. All seemed content. Imji developed a strange habit of walking around the edge of the circle, sometimes stopping to stare out beyond the parapet, apparently listening or scenting the air. What he learned by it no one asked him; and it was as well, for he would not have known how to answer.

In fact, no one was interested in asking. It was simply considered an odd habit, tolerated because he was respected enough to be granted the right to a little oddity. Less tolerable as time continued to pass was a growing restiveness among the younger members. Chief among these was Imji's former companion on the road. He was safe, secure, and bored. The parapet had become a prison and no longer a protection, a source of irritation. and discontent. He wanted to leave, and one day he told Imji, asking which of the roads leading from the circle he should take.

"It doesn't matter," replied Imji. "They all lead to other circles like this one."

"That is impossible," said the youngster hotly. "There must be something different, something more than this."

"They are all the same," said Imji. "I have made this journey seven times. They are all the same."

"Seven times or seventy," the youngster responded furiously, "I don't believe you. Have you tried every road there is?"

"No."

"Then I shall. You have given up, but I will not give up. I will take every road from this circle and every other until I find another place to be."

"There is no other place," said Imji again. "Only other circles just like this one."

In anger the young one wheeled and sprang away, not even bothering to choose

25

a road in his passion to be at least on one of them. His action infected others. Some followed him. There was a plunging, stamping confusion in the circle.

Only the elder and a few others remained calm. He knew that not many would leave. These occasional stampedes always passed, thinning out the young hotheads who would travel from one circle to another, gradually growing older and wiser, until, like Imji, they chose a place to remain. Some would always be restless, of course, and their future was written in the marks on the high wall that closed one section of the parapet.

Imji had never done more than wonder about that wall. It had a kind of frustrating attractiveness, but he was not the kind to be troubled by an obstacle he could get neither through nor over, and he wasted no time in desiring to penetrate it. It was there, and it was strange; a question he could not answer and accepted as such.

It came to him then as a shock when later he saw what could happen. Time had gone by, but how much time he did not know. One day his young companion of the road returned, not by the same route that he had left, and obviously young no longer.

He arrived at full gallop, sweating, and trembling with effort and fatigue. His gaze swept the circle and fell on Imji. Recognizing him, he realized that all his journeying had brought him not even to a similar circle, but to the very one he had left.

With a deep bellow of rage, he rushed for the wall as if by the very fury of his charge he could smash through it. With blood dripping from his head, he drew back and charged again—again and again in a total, impossible effort to force a way through to the only hope he saw remaining.

No one could stop him; and no one tried. They watched him break himself to pieces. When he was dead a group of them quietly removed him. The parapet was low enough for them to lift what remained and push it outside.

Imji remained motionless. He was trembling within his whole body, too stunned to move. He gazed at them all. But for an additional slight mark upon the wall, the circle was the same. Its inhabitants were occupying themselves in their accustomed manner. Apparently, nothing unusual had happened.

Without realizing what he did, Imji began to walk around the edge, unaware that his legs moved, seeing without knowing what he saw, listening and not knowing what he heard, unaware of any response to the scents on the air moving towards him from the trees. But he saw, he heard, and he responded. He kept walking, and gradually a new consciousness awoke in him. He was aware of the strange, terrible world behind the trees; he recalled its fears—but he also was listening to its voices.

Suddenly he stopped. All his senses were vividly alert in an instant of great clarity. He saw the circle and the roads. He saw the wilderness beyond the parapet. For a long moment he stood motionless. Then in one swift, beautiful leap, he lifted his strong body above the parapet and was gone into the darkness.

No one saw him go.

TRIVIA

E WAS a man of no importance. He was born, lived, and died, with no more permanent trace than a waterbird's passage down a canal. For a while, in the lifetime of his sons and his grandchildren, he was remembered, but eventually, time closed over the memory. His name was used among his descendants, as it had been among his ancestors, as a continuity without individual meaning, and in the end time closed over that too. The name, its meaning, and its roots were gone.

While he lived, not long, for he died in his thirties, he inhabited a small village in what for our time we call the Andes. He was a potter—his hands shaped the vessels in which his neighbors cooked, stored their corn, and lit their dwellings. His hands knew better than his words the texture and variety of clay, the depth of a glaze, the needed heat of a firing and its time span. His body knew what shapes and textures lent themselves to what purposes. In his work (not particularly original, for he had learned all this from his father and

grandfather) his hands were aware of the uses, and the meaning of these uses, of the things he made. As his fingers shaped a pot to store seed, they touched the hope of sowing time, frugality, greed, and also famine. A child of his died of hunger in one long winter. In cooking pots he touched the warmth of family fires and the companion-ship of those bound together for security, if not always for love. They touched the fu-neral feasts; cermonial meals accompany-ing death in which an attempt was made to ensure a connection of the living with the dead and a continuing of the one in the other. And there were the hands wet with tears on such occasions, at least once his own when his first young wife had died giving birth to their second child. Tears had moistened the clay for a while after that as his hands shaped new vessels, among them wine cups for a wedding. He had married again quite soon; his children needed a mother, and he needed more sons to help him and continue his name. Besides, he was an affectionate man, not meant to live alone, with love enough for more than one human being in his heart. If his new wife was not like his first; neither was his first like her.

The village was not often troubled by royal officials. It was out of the way and offered little. It was, nevertheless, subject to the labor tax which had not been demanded in the lifetime of any but the elders. Since to most of the village this had never happened, it had become something that would not happen. It was therefore both a shock and a grief when one day it did. The summons came, and ten of the younger men went away, further than they had ever dreamed of going before. Among them went the potter, not as young as the others but more knowledgeable about clay, to make bricks for the newest stage of the temple complex.

For him, more than for his companions, the work was frustrating. For them it was an unwanted interruption in their lives, performing an unwanted task until their allotted section of the wall was finished and they could return home. For him, accustomed to fashion the stuff he handled to the immediate purposes of living, the vast unseen design was meaningless, and to find himself endlessly emptying a wooden mold with the same square corners and the same straight lines was a limitation that slowly eroded him. His fingers had become the manner in which he lived and his life expressed itself in what he made. Life shrank to the dimensions of a brick.

Perhaps it is not surprising that he died. Certainly no one was surprised at the death of a workman. He was buried near the site with the others and his sons never managed to make the long journey to bring him home.

The required section of wall was finished, and for a time, it made part of the new complex. Eventually, in its turn, it was encased in a larger, higher level of building and was preserved at the core of the later structure. The temple mountain spread, grew tall, and then, like a tree, it slowly died. Gradually it withered; crumbled; and blew away to dust.

Another time came, in which none of this history was important, but in which people allowed their curiosity to dwell on strangely shaped, eroded hills. Some imaginations fashioned spacious, fallen halls, with treasures in the dark beneath, and they ripped the temple hill apart in search of forgotten wealth. Others came with a different passion to lay bare the meaning of the hill and stripped it in layers with the involved detachment of a surgeon penetrating a human body.

What had not blown away on many winds was exposed, core upon core, brick upon brick, and many more curious people came to stare and wonder, imagine, or just to pass the time in a different way. Among them one day came a woman seeking to make time pass in a different way because the ordinary way of its passing was too painful to endure much longer.

The bleak hill had little to attract attention and she walked away. The desolate plain around it was not much better: very little grew—a few thorny weeds struggling for life along shallow folds of ground whose regularity—so the guide had said—indicated that they once had been canals.

But the sun felt warm on her neck and the back of her hands, and the wind blew, somewhat gritty with dust. She stopped walking for a moment to concentrate on feeling it, soothing herself in the quiet of pure sensation. She felt dust on her neck and with a quick movement of annoyance or nervousness wiped it away with her hand. Then, for no good reason, she stooped, burying her hand in the dry soil, and let its grains run through her fingers as she scooped it up. It was a caressing gesture, but she was unconscious of it, staring without seeing at the worn hill and the clear, unshaped sky beyond.

She did not for the moment know where she was. She simply remained stooping, running the dry soil through her fingers, the expression on her face changing as the muscles around her eyes slowly relaxed. Her mind and thoughts quietly drifted and the wind blew on her neck.

A few moments passed. Eventually she came slowly to her feet and dusted off her hands. She walked about a little longer and wandered back to her party.

On the return journey, she felt the need to close her eyes and be silent. Gradually she became aware that something had changed. She did not know when it happened or how, but she was no longer alone.

THE
GODDESS

THE TEMPLE of the Goddess of Rest stood high on a hill, surrounded by gardens, and it was reached only after a long and weary journey by pilgrims who greatly desired to enter. Even then, the test of the journey was not enough. There was a special secret, a riddle, a proof, something that one must do before being admitted to her presence—no one quite knew what.

The Goddess of Rest was not like the other gods of the lands beyond the dawn. She did not seek out her worshipers, and she did not intervene in the doings of men. She had to be sought and what happened when she was found contained a mystery.

Two pilgrims who one day stumbled through the sloping gardens to her sanctuary were Adad and Geran. They had met upon the road and travelled together, shaping a friendship out of their common weariness and discouragement, helping one another to continue walking and accept yet another day of effort.

The gardens around the temple were cool and refreshing, shaded by trees, light-

ened by flowers, singing with falling waters. The ground still climbed steeply and neither Geran nor Adad wished to stop before they reached their goal. They greatly desired the presence of the Goddess.

They saw no one, but the path led clearly toward a high square archway giving entrance to an outer court. Through a secondary archway they passed to a space of pools and fountains and came to a high bronze door.

Now they felt afraid and hesitated. It was Geran, always a little the bolder of the two, who put out his hand to push open the door. It swung back easily in perfect balance, and the two men went through it into a long, wide hall in the quietness of which the shuffling of their rag-bound feet seemed a vulgar intrusion.

The hall was not dark. Light came through openings high in the wall and fell in rectangular patterns on a finely-veined marble floor. The walls were carved in shapes of vines and flowers so delicate that they seemed as if they would move in a breath of wind. It was very still. At the other end of the hall were two great doors of shimmering gold.

Slowly they advanced, gazing about them in awe, remembering tales about the tests that lay ahead. They were afraid to go forward and unwilling to go back.

The guardian seemed to appear from nowhere—yet he gave the impression of having been present all the time. Strangely, it was not a surprise to see him. He stood by the wall, quietly watching them approach. He appeared neither old nor young, and his face was composed in the kind of tranquillity that is near to a smile.

As they drew near, he bent his head to greet them and welcomed them by name. Again, strangely, they were not surprised.

"You wish to enter the presence of the Goddess," said the guardian, "and you know that you must first pass the test."

"We know," answered Geran, "and we are ready". His voice was not quite steady, whether from fear or eagerness.

"Are you?" said the guardian. "I hope so. It is not easy to see the Goddess. She is found only by those who search for her and choose her freely." Turning to Adad, he asked, "How would you know her?"

"Perhaps I would not," Adad replied. "She is in the silence at the heart of music; in the pause between two waves breaking on the shore. She is the space that passes beneath an archway, and is seen behind the outspread wing of a bird flying in the sunlight. She is found in the stillness around the edge of thought, the peace left behind by friendship, and in the ignorance of the very wise."

The guardian smiled and turned to Geran. "Do you agree?"

"No. I will say that she is the cessation of pain and the end of tormenting memory; a time of no more labor, no more fear. When exhaustion ends, insult is passed, and the long weight is lifted—then, and there, is Rest."

"He has answered well," said Adad.

"Then you say he is right?" said the guardian.

"Yes." Adad paused. "And yet . . . I, too, have answered well. I do not know."

The guardian said no more, but turned

away and walked towards the golden doors
at the end of the hall. Geran and Adad
looked uncertainly at one another and
awkwardly followed him, keenly aware of
their own smallness and shabbiness in
such a place. With a hand on the doors, the
guardian pushed them smoothly back,
then stood aside as if waiting for his guests
to pass.

A tall room was revealed with a roof
reaching up into darkness. At one end a
shallow flight of steps was flanked by smoking braziers and ended in a great stone
chair in which sat a veiled figure. The heavy
folds of its garments covered its feet. Its
arms were supported by the sides of the
chair and the ends of the fingers hung
down—long, white, bones without flesh.

Both men stood still upon the thresh-
old, waiting for a signal. The figure on the
throne-like chair did not move, nor did
the guardian. Looking at his face, they saw
that it was without expression, as if he were
gazing into a time that existed in a different
age. He did not seem to breathe. The silence grew so deep they could hear the

blood beat in their ears. Then Geran gave a sob and stepped tremblingly forward. A few more steps and he sank to his knees, weeping, his arms outstretched to the seated figure.

Adad turned away. His own eyes filled with tears and he ran blindly back down the great hall. The guardian must have moved with amazing speed for somehow his hand was on Adad's shoulder.

"Let me go," cried Adad, struggling against the grip.

"Not yet," replied the other. "Look around you."

Adad looked up and saw a smile in the guardian's eyes. The deep repose of his face impressed him as if he had never seen it before. He turned toward the door by which he had entered, but saw only light. The walls were dissolving in light—light itself in which nothing could be seen but its own essence, a refreshment and a delight that passed beyond the reach of vision to the source of his power of living.

Entranced, he did not know whether a moment passed or a hundred years. Then the light faded and the walls of the hall took shape once more. The guardian stood beside him and around him a clinging radiance still lingered.

"She is here," said Adad softly. "She is here."

"Yes. She is here."

The guardian led Adad slowly towards the doorway. "You have seen the Goddess," he said gently, "but now you must return to your own world, to live."

"But Geran?" said Adad. "I do not understand. Did he give the wrong answer?"

"You yourself said he answered well," replied the guardian. "But the test was not to know an answer; it was to know a question when it came."

TENOCHCANTITL

THE STEPS were high and beautiful—climbing steadily. The terraced stages of the ascent gradually narrowed to the central, vital point. Bright, whitened by the sun, they rose from the ground like something more than the earth could produce—a road to the sky.

There was a sound of lutes; the scent of flowers. Crowds in holiday garments had gathered, smiling, for this was a happy occasion. Bright blue in the ornaments of the women and gold in the armaments of the men caught the sunlight. A light breeze relieved the heat and set in motion the feathers of elaborate headdresses. They moved with a beauty of their own, yielding in unison but with their own individuality to the air, united with it and yet with a separate life. Vivid and vital, the crowd was happy, but tense, keyed to a moment of ordered anticipation.

Massed around the steps, rank upon rank, they had ceased to be precise but had found a superior order in their sheer numbers. None had dared to approach within

the sacred limits of the pyramid, but as close as they dared, they came to that white mountain of the gods, heart, mind, body, music, flowers, and gala robe concentrated on the lonely, white ascent.

Slowly a procession came. At the center walked a young man proud and handsome—a warrior in his bearing, but with no scars to prove it; the proof had been left on his enemies. Without blemish in his person or his honor, his bearing expressed the pride of life. His flower-crowned head was held high; his armor flashed with his stride. There was a smile on his lips and the expression of his eyes was that of a man who knew his worth—and knew it to be beyond price.

He and the procession of priests entered the empty space. They alone were worthy. But he alone was worthy to approach the steps. The priests moved back. Deliberately and proudly the young man moved forward. One garland he removed from his head and let it fall upon the first step before he dared—even he—dared to mount it. Then slowly, steadily, he climbed. One by one he left the garlands on the steps, a flute which he had carried and which he broke he left, the glittering armor, and the sword which he did not break but left still whole, unshattered, complete still and stained with no blood but that of the enemies of his people. The same people who watched him now.

White and beautiful, the steps climbed to the sun, and he climbed them. He alone dared climb, as he alone deserved; but there was one man who by right awaited him. Centuries of right lay behind the High Priest who stood at the pinnacle of the shrine awaiting the selected victim of the gods, the best of men.

And the best of men approached him, more worthy than any the High Priest could have chosen from his own people, a captive of war and thus a gift from the gods, a man who had proved it by slaying six of his greatest champions in ceremonial battle, a man who proved it now by the smile of triumph on his lips as he approached this culminating point of life.

Stripped now of garlands and ornaments, a man in youth and life, the victim stood before the priest. Both smiled, in welcome of the moment. On these two now much depended, not for only people or nation, but for the world, the universe.

More than happiness, more than joy, an ecstatic exultation possessed them both. The young man stretched himself out upon a plain white slab on the pinnacle of the steps. The old man raised the knife. The movement was swift, practiced, and a roar of joy and praise arose from the distant, tiny crowd as the priest raised towards the sun the still living, beating heart of the most worthy of men. As he held it in his hands, the throbbing stopped.

But it was enough. The heart still bled, but it was dead. The flesh on the sacrificial slab had twitched, then slumped to mere dead meat. It was over.

In order, with music, and with proper ritual, the crowd moved away. They broke into groups of families and friends, with time for gossip and for lighter things. For now they all knew—certainly—that for their generation and their children's, the sun would rise.

THE SLAVE

TA-AKRIT stood once more on the slave block, listening with satisfaction to the bidding. As a healthy, strongly muscled young man of sixteen, he had obviously become quite valuable merchandise. With any luck, he might find himself this time in a more congenial household. He had not enjoyed working in the stables of a horse dealer. Not that he disliked horses, but he disliked the smell. The distant memory of his mother, a body servant to a rich lady, whose hands had always carried the scent of the perfumed oils with which she massaged her mistress, must have spoiled him forever from stinking, dirty jobs. The bankruptcy of the lady's husband and consequent disposal of all saleable assets had separated Ta-Akrit from those early memories and launched him on a succession of menial and disagreeable tasks. Now, however, he was likely to fetch a price which would assure him more attractive surroundings. The only danger was that he might attract the fancy of one of the masters' women,

and any slave of his age knew that meant trouble—one way or another.

He tried to follow the bidding, to guess who was likely to get him, but he was not familiar enough with the agents to know. The prices were coming fast and sufficiently high to be reassuring, but the rapid speech of the auctioneer was too difficult to follow. The gong sounded unexpectedly, announcing the sale. He was led from the block, still unsure who had bought him.

He was placed with a group of strong young men like himself and had a sudden fear that they had been selected for a factory. Then two girls joined them and he felt relieved. "Where are we going?" he whispered to one of them (you could usually trust the women to have sharp noses). "I'm not sure," she replied, "but I think it is one of the temples." Better and better, thought Ta-Akrit; plenty of good food, and so many slaves that no one will have to work too hard. No fear of bankruptcy either. Of course, one might still end up looking after sacred chariots or cleaning a pool of hippopotami, but there were enough pleasant spots if a man were lucky enough or wily enough to get one of them. The girls were probably weavers, or perhaps even dancers. One of them at least was quite pretty. He looked at her again. Very pretty.

So it was with feelings of pleasant anticipation that Ta-Akrit entered the Temple of Amun and had his name changed to Amenakrit, since he was now the property of the god. His first tasks were not heavy, chiefly ceremonial in character. He frequently was a fan-bearer near the god, and since Amun did not perspire, this was no great task. The complex ritual of the god's service, however, which occupied a couple of thousand people daily, was at first entirely bewildering. He frequently became lost in the temple's outbuildings. He eventually learned how to find his way between his sleeping quarters, the scene of his duties, and his mess, and from these basic points gradually took in the rest. At the end of a year, he knew most of what went on and where: the storage rooms and treasury, the places where the clerks and accountants worked, the master builders and craftsmen who maintained the building in its splendid perfection, the weavers who made robes for the god and his priests and the less skilled who provided for the household, the dancers, the cooks, the priests' quarters and their families, the school—the temple was a city, a self-contained civilization, and it became his familiar home.

One ceremony that never ceased to fascinate him was the procession of the god at festivals. Amun was carried in an ornate palanquin on the shoulders of young men (who were no more strong or well made than Amenakrit) through an adoring throng of worshipers. These bearers walked on fresh blossoms strewn in the god's path by young girls, they breathed the burning perfumes offered him, and heard in their ears the shouts of adulation. This was the task Amenakrit desired.

The god was no mere passenger, however. He could make known his will. At times his palaquin would grow so heavy that the bearers staggered to the ground beneath it, and until Amun's wishes were ascertained by the priests and carried out, he remained where he was and no power of man sufficed to raise him. Such occasions were greeted with both fear and rejoicing; fear of displeasing the god and rejoicing that he had made known his presence.

One day this very event occurred just as Amun was re-entering his sanctuary, right at the point where Amenakrit stood holding a flaming torch with which he was about to escort the god to the cool shade of his throne. The palanquin sank unsteadily to the ground as the bearers' strength proved insufficient against its sudden weight. One man in particular must have crumpled in an unusually strange position, or the weight pressed on him more unequally than on the others, for his face was distorted with pain and he moaned.

Amenakrit, born a slave, knew better than to step unbidden from his assigned place, particularly in, of all places, the temple of Amun. But whether from pity for the man, from desire to take his place, or for some other reason he never had time to think about, he placed his torch in the socket on the wall behind him and moved towards the poles of the palanquin. He lifted it from the trapped man and it came easily. Feeling the sudden lightness, the other bearers rose, and with Amenakrit they carried the god to his shrine. He seemed to weigh no more than the golden feathers of his headdress.

Amun had obviously selected another bearer personally, so there could be no question of flogging Amenakrit to death for impiety. And Amun continued to choose Amenakrit as his bearer. An attempt to replace him eight years later with a younger man was prevented when the god refused to budge until Amenakrit returned to his customary position. Amun made his wishes known even more forcibly on a second occasion when he crushed the chest of the replacement and required that Amenakrit be dragged from his bed in a fever to bear him in procession. This time Amenakrit did not appreciate the honor quite as much. When well and strong, it was not a great distress to be forced to his knees or even flat to the ground when the god chose to indicate his pleasure. These moments were not frequent, and it was rare that the weight was so crushing as to be painful. And there was the perfume and the shouts and the excitement. There was, above all, the knowledge that he was personally selected as the slave of the god. However, with a fever, a head that felt as if it would roll off if he moved it, and legs that could not bear his own weight, even the ordinary burden of the palanquin was a torture. For the first time, Amenakrit wished that Amun had chosen someone else.

Years continued, and Amenakrit grew slowly older and more tired. At times he was ill. But the god had a god's unawareness of human ills and demanded still the services of his honored and selected bearer. Others came and went and were replaced, but never Amenakrit. Amun would not move without him. To bear him became a steadily increasing weight and weariness, one which the slave came more and more to dread. When the palanquin forced him to the ground he would close his eyes and wish never to rise again, and at times the force was so intolerable that he both feared and hoped that it would kill him. His life began to center around one longing: to escape from Amun.

From time to time Amun would leave his temple and go on great progresses through other cities and even subject provinces. The local governors and princes fell over each other to do him honor and thus disprove the lies their petty rivals were telling Pharoah about their dealings with the Hittite Emperor or the sea pirates. Amenakrit had never been a fool, and as a child in the service of a merchant, he had learned the businessman's Akkadian and the most widespread of the Hittite languages. Standing like a statue near the statue of the god, he had heard much that these princelings should have been wiser than to say. He was better equipped than most to fend for himself outside the domain of Amun, and a plan began to take shape in his mind.

So it was that when Amun was next

aboard his barge to sail the Upper Nile, Ta-Akrit slipped overboard and two days later was on a ship bound for northern Canaan. He made his way to Alalakh, a city which he knew was at that time strongly within the Hittite alliance and where he would not have to fear the reach of Amun. He found work there grooming horses. His new master certainly suspected him of being a runaway slave, but as that enabled him to pay lower wages, he was careful to believe Ta-Akrit's tale of having escaped from pirates.

Amun was left without his bearer, and if he wished to move at all, had to accept a substitute. He certainly moved. He made his progresses through Egypt, and even into Canaan, but did not come as far north as Alalakh. Ta-Akrit heard of them with greedy interest and fear, and heard also that on these occasions the god was not always treated with respect. This irritated Amun's ex-slave, who thought he would have enjoyed being a witness or even taking part in such a scene. Occasionally, he even found himself wishing that Amun would visit Alalakh and see how the Hittite sympathizers would greet him.

It was the last thing that seemed likely to happen, but, as is the fortunes of gods and men, the unlikely happened. Two great armies met at Kadesh, where armies had met many times before, and having failed by the usual mixture of blunders and good luck to annihilate each other, parted with the usual face-saving claim that each had won an overwhelming victory. A carefully worded treaty ratified the non-conclusion, spelling out various ceremonial gestures that would present the proper appearances to each side without altering realities in the slightest. And so—Amun was to come to Alalakh.

He came, and Ta-Akrit was in the crowd. The inhabitants of Alalakh were curious. The political considerations that were so real to their masters were non-existent to them, and at the moment they did not particularly care for Egyptians or their gods. However, if it meant some profits and no trouble, they were willing enough to

enjoy a holiday. Amun's reception, therefore, was less than adoring, but not insult-
ing. A few sneering remarks were heard, but
merchants had no objections to a procession which used their wares and there was
an adequate amount of cheerful noise.

Ta-Akrit was disappointed. He had
hoped to see Amun despised and humili-
ated. True, he was not being worshipped,
but that was not enough. Perhaps one of
the bearers would trip and pitch the god
into the street. The procession reached the
point where he was standing and one of
the bearers tripped. He fell. The palanquin
lurched to the ground. The yell Ta-Akrit
had hoped for went up from the crowd.
Amun had not been tipped into the street,
but his chair was on the ground and the
bearers were struggling helplessly to raise
it.

Ta-Akrit recognized the familiar signs,
but the crowd did not. Amun seemed helpless and was surrounded with catcalls and
jeers. Ta-Akrit stood listening to them with
a mounting anger against these Asiatic
fools who did not realize what was happen-

ing or know the power they were offending. Impatiently, the old slave of nearly sixty pushed his way through the crowd. It was a struggle to get through the tangle of arms and legs, and he was panting as he bent over the pole of the man who had tripped.

He lifted the pole easily and the palanquin swung lightly up to the shoulders of the bearers. Amun seemed to weigh no more than the feathers of his headdress.

Ta-Akrit and Amun moved on together. The bearer paid no more attention to the crowd than did the statue. He had deserved death for his escape, but they would not kill him, for Amun would not permit it. He would continue to bear Amun through illness, exhaustion, and death, and after death Amun would insist upon him as his bearer in the underworld. He was Amenakrit; Amun's slave forever.

THE
BENKLI

Mr. KOBUSHYERE was the type of man an emerging nation both needed and appreciated. He was well aware of how much he was needed and had received satisfactorily tangible proofs of the appreciation. Having been educated at one of the universities of an older and declining world, he combined the best of two eras—at the price, alas, of loneliness. While his intellectual associates had been too cynical to believe that a nation could avoid the errors into which their societies had fallen and had been unable to appreciate his vigor, his compatriots were too crude to share his sophistication and had a regrettable tendency to over-simplify complex problems.

He sighed as he gazed around the table at which his subordinates were seated—all able men in their way, of course. Such burdens were the penalty of greatness, and it was the mark of greatness to be willing to pay it. He gathered himself together and opened the meeting.

The problem, he explained, was that their particular department was perhaps a

little too much in advance of the times to have won an adequate measure of popular approval. (His pet project, for which his own preferred term was "productive re-habilitation", was known to the press as "human recycling" and to the irreverent in government circles as "the sewage center".) While the eminent scientists and social servants seated beside him were well aware of the value of their experiments in psycho-surgical medicine and re-education, thereby turning social misfits into acceptable citizens, the uneducated taxpayer had yet to be convinced that the results achieved were worth the cost. The general election was only a year away, and naturally economic conditions would be a major factor in the outcome. The Minister of Human Resources did not have to remind his distinguished listeners of the complexities of the situation.

He paused. He knew he was quite safe in assuming that no one would ask awkward questions about the complexities, and also that they all translated his remarks correctly. Some of the eminent scientists lured from decadent universities by the double temptation of high salaries and unlimited freedom—almost—to experiment had begun to look more lofty and indifferent than usual. Some of his own people were shifting uneasily.

There was unfortunately no doubt, he continued, that the Opposition would insist upon closing down the department, since they had already condemned it as a waste of public money.

It would be tragic, the Minister went on, if the world's most enlightened experiment in social rehabilitation should have to founder upon the rock of public ignorance, and he was personally willing and eager to lend an open ear to any imaginative solution that would contribute to raising the general level of appreciation of the value of this important endeavor and thus enable it to continue.

For the next ten minutes Mr. Kobushyere withdrew to a contemplative distance from the flood of sounds which his statement had released and allowed the cacophany of self-justification and complaints to flow past him. When he had had enough, he glanced at his Deputy, a pale-complexioned young man of impassive countenance and sharp eyes with a brutal, but useful, habit of getting straight to the point.

"If I have understood His Excellency correctly," said the Deputy, making himself heard by his usual simple methods, "what the situation demands is one outstanding example, a 'model' success, which we can show to the country as a proof of our usefulness."

"But the statistics," moaned a European scientist, "the statistics of adaptation from tribal to urban life are already very impressive."

"Statistics, Herr Doktor," said the Deputy, are not good press. They are nothing compared to photographs of a real man. That is what we need—a real man—before and after—visible proof of an outstanding transformation. Nothing less than that will convince the voters."

"Or the Budget Director," muttered an unidentified but audible voice.

"I am afraid I have to agree," intervened

the Minister before the noise could break out again. "While we must all deplore the necessity, it would appear to be more expedient at the moment for us to abandon other projects in order to concentrate all our talents—all these extraordinary talents," he repeated with a graceful gesture around the room, "on one peerless example of rehabilitation which will captivate the hearts and minds of our people, and ..."

"All right, all right," said a testy voice, interrupting what was obviously the start of another speech. "Who do we pick, and what do we do with him?"

"Obvious!" said another with a snort of laughter. "Since money's the problem, money's the answer. Let's make a Minister of Finance. We have the brain of an international embezzler in storage. Should be perfect."

Mr. Kobushyere closed his eyes and repressed a shudder. When these westerners chose to be crude, they were incredibly crude. They had no comprehension of the subtle tributes that were due to principles that one might—lamentably—be obliged to lay aside for the moment. The Deputy did not share his sensitivity. It was plainly a good idea.

"Are you sure you can do it?" he asked.

After a brief pause of silent reproof the men around the table assured him stiffly that of course they could do it.

"Then, if His Excellency approves, it remains only to pick the subject. May I suggest, Sir, that one of the villages around Lake Miasa might provide a suitable candidate."

"Lake Miasa! Surely we are not involved with that area?"

"Not yet, Sir," replied the Deputy, "but the Minister of Defense plans to begin clearing the region for a military air base in about four months and it would be as well to be a step ahead of the . . . that is to say, a selection in that area would demonstrate our foresight and intelligent anticipation of future need. Besides," he went on, lapsing a little, "they are a terribly backward lot and look almost half-witted. The photographs would be very impressive. Shouldn't be surprised if the story made the international front pages."

Mr. Kobushyere tried not to brighten visibly. "The suggestion certainly has merit and I will give it very thorough consideration." He looked around the room. "If there is nothing more to add, then, gentlemen, we will adjourn."

Three weeks later an old man shuffled into Mr. Kobushyere's office looking more bewildered than afraid. Two days of totally strange sights and sounds bombarding his senses at high speed had reduced him to a level of exhaustion at which he could no longer think. Three days ago he had been beside Lake Miasa, listening to the speech of the grasses and reading the ripples on the water. Since then he had been carried at dizzy speeds and at heights that made him sick, to a place of stones instead of trees, of painful noise, and things that rushed at one another in straight lines but somehow never met.

He heard Mr. Kobushyere with difficulty. The Minister's words and accent were at times unintelligible, but the old man did his courteous best not to convey this to the stranger. He gathered more from the gesture than the speech that he was to be seated. With quiet but painful dignity, he approached a chair and folded his legs beneath him on its seat.

Mr. Kobushyere by this time was growing tired and annoyed. He was at his tenth interview that morning in search of a candidate for the great experiment and was perfectly ready to agree with his Deputy that the Lake Miasa people were a half-witted lot. They represented the kind of past his country had to eradicate. He wondered for the tenth time why he had allowed himself to become personally involved in the selection. He heard himself give the usual explanation of why the villagers were to be moved from their present home and how an enlightened and progressive government was ready to give them every assistance they needed to make an easy transition to the new type of life they were to enter. He doubted whether the old man understood a word of it.

Obviously, the old man didn't. He said politely that he simply wished to return to his village.

Mr. Kobushyere explained the advantages of a progressive civilization and the role that his—their country was destined to play in the world. He was very good at this; it was a beautiful speech.

The old man said again that he just wanted to return to his village.

Exasperated, Mr. Kobushyere gave it up.

"Well, you can't," he snapped. "The village will not exist in a few months. You have to adapt to a new life, and we are going to help you do it. What skills do you have? Were you a fisherman? a boat maker? What were you?"

But the old man was apparently unable to comprehend more than the fact that for some reason his village was going to be destroyed, and Mr. Kobushyere had to spend a wearisome quarter of an hour on this before he could get an answer to his question. Finally the old man said he was the village witch doctor.

"Not witch doctor!" said an irritated

Minister. "Guru. Mystical teacher—but not witch doctor. We are not a lot of savages. What actually did you do?"

"I sang; danced; made people well."

"You sang, danced? Well, there may be some cultural value in that. Let me see you."

The old man explained that it was impossible. He sang with the voices of the water and danced with the movement of the trees. Without the lake and the trees it was impossible to sing or dance. Besides he could only do so when the Benkli danced and sang with him.

"Benkli! What's a benkli?" demanded Mr. Kobushyere.

The old man fumbled in the unaccustomed pockets of the coat someone had wrapped him up in and produced an odd piece of wood. He held it reverently in his hands and placed it on the desk.

"This is my Benkli," he said. "I make Benklis—I have made them for many villages. But this is my own Benkli."

The Minister of Human Resources looked at the object before him. It was a crudely carved, semi-abstract, semi-human figure with a face of sorts. It had no artistic merit.

He sighed. "You have no skills or trade, and this thing is of no value whatever."

He looked thoughtfully at the old man. A more useless social reject he could not imagine. An ideal candidate if something could be done with him. But could anything be done? It would take a miracle. No, not a miracle, he thought to himself with pleasure—a challenge. A magnificent challenge to his very superior scientists to prove their words.

It was in this way that the old man, whose name no one bothered to ask, was chosen as the object of the greatest experiment that the Department of Productive Rehabilitation had ever attempted. He was told, but probably never heard, that he was about to make a great contribution to the welfare of his people and of mankind and taken from the room. He was too proud to weep or to attempt to regain the Benkli which the Minister had firmly retained. He moved out of the room with the same dignity and the same quiet bewilderment with which he had entered it.

Mr. Kobushyere had kept the Benkli only to emphasize that the old man must abandon his past and move ahead to his future. He placed it on his desk and forgot it.

A few days later his Deputy brought him the first reports on the Lake Miasa experiment. The scientists were surprisingly enthusiastic. Although intelligence testing rated the subject at the level of a backward pre-adolescent, the witch doctor's brain showed unusual development in certain areas. To the Deputy the most outstanding point was that instead of being in his sixties, he was merely a devitaminized forty: the photographs would be superb.

The Benkli on the Minister's desk now assumed the character of a symbol of approaching triumph. And it was a triumph—the greatest of Mr. Kobushyere's career. All the resources of his exhausted staff, their talents and energies, some of the most expensive components they had in storage (a mathematician of genius, a famous actor, a PR man—not to mention the embezzler), their most advanced equipment and techniques, had within six months turned the witch doctor into Mr. Gihar Beniakim, a distinguished man with just the right touch of grey in his hair, a man of fluent speech, devastating logic, and convincing tact. Mr. Beniakim retained the dignity of his former self but added to it an air of assurance and the gift of being rude when he chose. The Benkli was given a place of honor in Mr. Kobushyere's office.

Gihar Beniakim's rise to prominence was swift. An introduction to the President resulted in a post as special economic adviser. He campaigned brilliantly in the elections of the following year and won a seat in Parliament, rising soon thereafter to a place in the Cabinet. Within two years he was well known in international banking circles and within three to the international press. He became a world figure.

The Benkli continued to reign in its incongruous setting in Mr. Kobushyere's office, crudely prominent in the otherwise artistic surroundings. The Minister of

Human Resources refused to part with him. The Benkli was concrete evidence of his greatest achievement and he felt a justifiable pleasure whenever he looked at it. He looked at it often. When his mind wandered he would find that his eyes were resting on it; it was the first thing he looked for on entering his office and it gave him a feeling that a man less aware of his own value might have mistaken for reassurance.

As time went on, people noticed that the Minister's mind wandered quite often and his eyes strayed to the Benkli more and more. It was sometimes difficult to recall his attention to the matter in hand. Work in his office was slowing down. Mr. Kobushyere was not aware of this, but he was aware of a growing feeling of discomfort which was relieved when he entered the office and saw the Benkli in its accustomed place. He became steadily more conscious of some kind of link with the ridiculous object, which was at first irritating and by imperceptible stages became frightening.

That he was afraid finally dawned on

him at a meeting with his staff. In the middle of one of his smooth sentences, he suddenly felt as if a wall had come down between him and the other persons in the room. Through the wall he could see them, hear them, talk to them, probably touch them if he tried, but he was not in contact with them. He was cut off. He looked across the room at the Benkli and realized that it was on the same side of the wall as himself. The two of them were together in a world to which no one else had access. Fear built up in him slowly as he forced his mind to pay attention to the sights and sounds around him. They were vivid and clear, but their very sharpness increased the horrible sense of isolation.

The feeling passed but left him shaken. It took him a couple of days to talk himself back into a rational condition, and he had just succeeded when it happened again. This time he was in his car and quite alone but for his chauffeur. The world around him retreated from his presence, though not from his consciousness, and he was left in a horrifying solitude from which he could not reach out. Appalled, he ordered his car back to the ministry and ran to his office. Without thinking, and almost sobbing, he snatched up the Benkli and was immediately aware of its contact.

From that moment he never let it out of his reach. The periods of isolation grew longer and more frequent, and the Benkli was the only thing that could accompany him into them. It offered no warm companionship; at times its presence even felt hostile, but at least it was a presence. Soon Mr. Kobushyere was existing almost continually in a double world, the one he could clearly perceive but could not enter, and the one in which he actually lived with the Benkli. With deepening horror he came to realize that the Benkli was not entering his world, he was entering the Benkli's. He would have destroyed it if he could; but he dared not run the risk of being alone.

The Benkli began to assume control. It took him into forests and made him listen to the trees; into lakes where he felt the currents of deep water; and eventually to oceans where no man had ever been, where he saw creatures no light had ever reached and heard the songs they made to one another. The Benkli tried to make him express these sounds and movements, and moments stretched into agony as Mr. Kobushyere fought against it. He gripped his desk with sweating hands as he attempted to answer a subordinate's question and heard his own voice croaking an unintelligible song. In spite of himself he swayed and moved as the Benkli took possession of him, and through his body and his mind entered the man's world of being.

The efficient Deputy Minister issued a press release stating that Mr. Kobushyere had suffered a heart attack. This was soon followed by the announcement of his retirement for reasons of ill health. He was removed to a discreet nursing home where, after the usual number of tributes to his many years of devoted public service, he was rapidly forgotten.

But the Benkli was not finished with him. It had further worlds to show him and make him express, worlds that no man could ever have known. Mr. Kobushyere walked through towering growths that had existed before any man was born to see them, and had his spirit torn to shreds by winds that had eroded stars. He could no longer fight to reach another human being, because none existed in such places. He was alone without hope of ever being otherwise—except for the presence of the Benkli.

He had thought there could be nothing worse; but he was wrong. The Benkli took him to places where men had been or would one day be. He saw their shattered gods and felt what only men can feel: the eternal, uneased pain of a thousand generations of useless effort. He saw blighted fields and felt the hunger of a million years. He saw cities built, destroyed, and built again, and was forced to die, come back to life, hope, and die again. He was not allowed the luxury of despair, but was compelled to endure the joy and hope of countless births. He felt friendships and loss, and the longings for another day. The whole reality of existence and mankind was pressed upon him and demanded to be heard through him. He was shattered by its power, but not allowed to want to die.

Mr. Kobushyere had been a man of very robust constitution. It took five years for the strain to kill him. As he was dying, he remembered an old man who once had said that he sang with the voices of the water and danced with the movement of the trees, but only when the Benkli sang and danced with him. To the nurse beside him it seemed that he briefly recovered lucidity before the end. He asked that the ugly wooden object from which he had always refused to be parted be given to Mr. Gihar Beniakim in remembrance of him.

The distinguished financier took the Benkli reverently and lovingly into his hands. Tears streamed down his face, and his assistant heard him murmur, "It is too late, my friend. They have separated us for ever."

The remark was interpreted in the press as a tribute to his dead benefactor.

PEVENSEY

I

A SOUTHWEST wind was raising white crests on the sea and blowing spray into Vredicca's face as she walked by the shore. She could taste salt on her lips. She loved days like this, when the clouds moved fast above her head and the grey sky and grey sea seemed to meet and become one in a wild union that included her in its freedom. Moist and fresh, the wind blew through her long, dark hair and whipped her robe around her. She enjoyed the billowing resistance of her cloak as she drew it closer. The heavy gold pin fastening it to her shoulder had been dragged round her neck. She looked and felt as she could rarely feel these days, daughter and wife of chieftains, proud and free as the sea and the wind that owned no mastery but their own.

Vredicca walked along the shore, then turned inland a little to the long, low mound where her grandfather's body lay. It was now the only place where she belonged—with the dead. It was the only place where bitterness was eased and loneliness put to rest. She watched the wind blowing through the grass and wished that it could blow likewise through her, through spirit and flesh, bearing her away and scattering her over the land as it did the seeds of the grass, one with the wind and one at rest with the land.

She stood looking down on the burial mound, then looked westward to where the long, grey promontory stretched out into the sea like a gigantic warship. On clear days it gleamed white, a long line of white cliff thrusting out into the water with a green line of grass above it. On those cliffs her grandfather had once stood, with massed chariots behind him, watching the real warships below. He had seen long ships with banks of oars, seen the glint of sun on armor, and standards surmounted by the long-expected sign of the eagles. He had watched them round the cliffs and ordered his men to follow as they went eastward on a rough sea. Ships and chariots had together moved along the shore, watching each other, until the

Roman warships had rowed too far away to be any longer a threat to his people.

He had seen them go past, thought Vredicca, but he had not seen them return. He had been sleeping a long time in his green mound when they came back. He had stood ready to fight, to kill and to die, when Caesar came with his ships. When Vespasian came with his legion, her own son had submitted. What would the old man have thought? What would he have thought of her grandson, returned from his Roman education, shaved like a fop, skirted like a woman, perfumed and mincing, hardly able to understand Belgic, and shuddering affectedly at the customs of his own homeland?

Vredicca wished passionately that she too had died before the world had been wiped away, wished that she had never given birth to those who had brought about this transformation. The heritage she knew—the tales, the pride, the courage— were buried now in the grass. It was her work to transmit the gifts of many generations to her heirs, but those gifts had been struck from her hands with light witticisms in a language she did not even wish to understand. Her life had been a long travail to give birth to a dead child.

II

The Count of the Saxon Shore struck the wall with his fist in exasperation.

"Careful, Sir," the Fort Commander remarked grimly. "It might fall down."

Since the wall in question was eight feet thick, this was hardly likely, but the Count saw nothing funny in the remark. The walls were in a shocking state of disrepair and to his experienced—and at that moment, pessimistic—eye, the weakest point of all, the gate, could be forced by ten determined men.

"This place hasn't been repaired in fifty years. Why has no one ever worked on it?"

"Because we never had the men."

Count Aulius knew the answer before he asked the question; knew too that he had no business even asking it. He was the man responsible for the forts. They were decaying when he took on the task from his father and he had helplessly watched their further disintegration over the years. He was talking only to relieve a frustration approaching despair.

"There seem to be plenty of men here now," he snapped.

"They are from my villa at Becslunum," said the other.

Count Aulius was brought up short. "I'm sorry, Caballus," he said. "I wasn't thinking."

He had underlined his apology with the use of his friend's nickname and the older man accepted it by swiftly touching the Count's shoulder and turning away. Both stood silent for a moment, looking out to sea.

"There's no harvest left for them to reap, no house to care for, no livestock. Ashes can look after themselves—so can the dead. They are more use here. But don't expect too much," Caballus added. "There isn't a soldier among them. They are all farmers."

That was the trouble, Aulius thought bitterly. No soldiers. In his grandfather's time, the Count of the Saxon Shore commanded a legion. He could man forts that provided ·an armored chain of protection along the coast from here in Anderida all the way eastward to the Thames. German raiders had struck nonetheless, but for two hundred years they had been compelled to approach their victims with a wary stealth that betokened respect.

Not now. Now the legions were long gone. Rome's frontier ran not through Britain but through Gaul. The legions were gone to protect the latest edge of civilization far to the south, and here they were left, an isolated, amputated outpost, with only a strip of sea and a line of crumbling, unmanned forts to protect them from the flaming ruin that had already destroyed half of Europe.

Count Aulius had inherited the title and the task, but none of the means with which to perform it. His father had faced the same problem and finally ceased even to appeal to Rome for men. But between his farms and his library he had found enough to content him and to reinforce the philosophical trend of his mind, so that he came to contemplate the eventual possibility of an end to the Empire with stoic fortitude.

Easy enough to face an intellectual possibility, thought Aulius, but now the flames were only seven miles away at Becslunum and Anderida was the last of the forts. His father had seen the raids increase, known the growing boldness and intensity of Saxon attacks. Even in his lifetime they were coming in packs of twenty ships, already bringing their wives and children with them and had made their first permanent encampment. Surely his father had seen a man with the same expression on his face as Caballus had now? How had he maintained his philosophic calm? Or had he managed to disbelieve that the end could really come?

Caballus broke the silence.

"You did not bring the Lady Albia with you?"

"No," replied Aulius. "I have sent her west with the whole household. Her brother is at Caerleon and she will be safe there."

Caballus grunted in reply and wiped his nose on his tunic. Aulius thought he had condemned his father too quickly: one can endure another man's grief. His own wife was in safety; Caballus' family was dead.

"Before long we may have to go as far as Hibernia or Caledonia," Caballus said bitterly. "Perhaps we should all have left for Rome."

"That was too late a long time ago. Besides we don't belong in Rome, my friend. Our fathers were here before the legions came, and our sons will be here after even these Saxons have gone."

"Not my sons," said Caballus, and Aulius bit his lip. "You sound like your father. But you're right. We belong here."

They fell silent again, standing together on the wall and looking to the horizon. To the west, the white headland thrust itself out into the water like a spear. The sea was blue with a rippling glitter of sunlight. A soft, moist wind blew out their cloaks, blew through the marshy grasses where cattle grazed and on over scattered mounds into the thick woods behind. There was a hum of bees and a splash of water against the walls.

The angry frustration had passed over Aulius like the crest of a wave, leaving him in a trough of hopelessness. Now there was only one task left: to meet the end like a man. Calmly he stood looking out across the water, waiting for the ships to come.

III

How could spring come this year, thought Aedgitha. She stood outside the door of the old house and looked down the street. There was a sharp, brisk wind snapping at her cloak, but the sun was shining and crocuses were already showing their heads. The wind was blowing too much spray for Beachy Head to be clearly seen, but the cliff gleamed white when it occasionally revealed itself. There was something of excitement and of life in the wind that was wrong. How could spring come when Eric was dead? As if to contradict her mood, the child kicked in her belly.

She looked to her right, a half a mile away, to the ancient ring of grass-grown stone and the mound within it. It was a place the village had always shunned, a place full of ghosts. The tales said a great battle had been fought there and the slain lay unburied until the grass rose and covered them. It was a long time ago, but there were people who said the dead were not at rest and still walked at times on those broken walls or could be seen standing looking out to sea. Aedgitha had always feared the place till now. But now there had been another battle and Eric was dead. He had been buried and put to rest behind the Church, but Aedgitha could understand if he too walked along the shore or looked out to sea. Perhaps he and those restless spirits of long ago were comrades now.

The child stirred again and reminded Aedgitha of her present problem. What was she going to do? The choice before her would have seemed fantastic a year ago when she and Eric married. He was the oldest son of a metalsmith who did a thriving trade in fine work. At one time, long ago, before there was one kingdom in England, they had been moneyers for the King of Wessex. The old mint was still part of the house, but they made ornaments there now, not coins: buckles and shoulder pins, decorated spearheads and heavy collars.

Aedgitha turned eastward and walked out of the village by the shore. The wind was raising white crests on the sea. Would this be the future for Eric's child or not? It had appeared certain until last October when the dragon-headed ships pulled up on the beach. Long before King Harold's exhausted men had made their forced march southward from resounding victory to final defeat, Eric was dead. He had tried to reach Harold with news of William's landing and a Norman arrow killed him before he gained the trees.

She walked along the shore and turned slightly inland to the place where Eric had died. There was no mark on the ground and the wind blew through the grass here just as it blew elsewhere. Only her memory marked the spot.

The wind blew round her too, whipping her dark hair over her face. Eric had loved her hair and teased her. He said he loved small, dark women, and suspected she came on a trader's slave ship from the east. (As metalsmiths his family knew many traders and their tales of distant places.) She had been indignant and told him that her people had been millers at Bexlei for as long as his had been minters in Pevensey. He had laughed and said that made her a foreigner anyway for Bexlei was seven miles off. Who knew what strange people came from Bexlei?

He would not have known, for they had not met in Bexlei which he had never seen in his life. They had met at Hurst, further inland, where she had been tirewoman to the young Lady Edith and he had come, at special order, to show some jewelry to the elderly Lady of Hurst. Both Adegitha and Eric were in fact quite well travelled, which was an additional attraction between them.

But the journey offered her now was another story. Much had happened since that terrible October. The battle was over, and the King was dead. The Wotan had made William king and crowned him in December. A Norman Abbey was rising on the spot where Harold's standard fell, and Norman laws and Norman ways were already felt. Eric's father had stood aloof from the battle in spite of his son's death and said that kings were none of his making or his care. The next brother to Eric, Rolf, said the same. But the youngest, Leofwyne, had fought at Senlac, and it was not to be expected that vengeance would not soon seek him out. Leofwyne did not intend to wait for it. He planned to take ship with a merchant to Constantinople and enter the service of the Eastern Emperor. Fabulous tales were told of that distant, golden city, and it was rumoured that others were going too. Leofwyne's wife was with child also, and he urged Aedgitha to come with them, so that his son and Eric's might grow up in their own ways and not as Normans.

"Better to grow up as Greeks?" said Aedgitha, her common sense asserting itself.

What did freedom mean in other than a Saxon world?

"Yes," said Leofwyne. "At least the Greeks did not kill Eric, and our sons can choose. Here they cannot choose."

Aedgitha was no nearer a decision now than ever. She simply wished that spring would not come, the child would not grow, and that time would go back to before the ships had come, to when she and Eric had walked hand in hand along this shore, breathing the air as if it were life itself and eternal, a world of happiness that could not end. How could she leave this place where life had been so much and where Eric died?

She walked back to the house and to her surprise saw a litter drawn up outside. She went in to find the Lady Edith of Hurst seated by the smoking hearth. Lady Edith rose and ran to take her in her arms.

Aedgitha was confused. She tried to curtsey, couldn't, then attempted to make her former mistress sit down and compose herself. Finally seated and looking at her, Aedgitha was shocked to see that once beautiful young face so much older and drawn into lines that would soon become permanent. The shining fair hair was disshevelled and her eyes rimmed with red.

"My lady," stammered Aedgitha. "My Lady Hurst."

"No," cut in Edith. "Not the Lady of Hurst. The Dame de Monceaux."

There was a silence of pure astonishment. Aedgitha's father-in-law and his sons did not comprehend and Aedgitha was afraid to.

The Lady Edith continued. "I am the last of my family, and the King—King William—has given me in marriage to his faithful knight, the Sieur de Monceaux."

"But . . ." Aedgitha hesitated. "Lord Edwin . . ."

"Edwin was the only one of my brothers to survive the battle at Senlac. He has gone . . . I think to the north . . . and is declared outlaw."

No further explanation was needed. Lady Edith's brother could already be dead; he might as well be. The only one left of the family that had wielded authority for five centuries was this girl. She was married to one of William's knights and so would secure for him and his descendants the legitimate fidelity of her family's adherents. That it had been necessary to kill her father and brothers in the process did not matter. Her sons would be the heirs of thirty generations of loyalty and they would also be true Normans, faithful to their king.

"Aedgitha," said Lady Edith. "Come back with me. I shall bear sons who will be reared as Norman knights; who will not know my father's language. Be someone with me to whom I can speak in my own tongue. I shall not be allowed to tell my children of their father's deeds, but we can tell yours. Let your child inherit what I cannot give my own—the heritage your husband and my brothers died for."

Aedgitha accompanied the Lady Edith back to Hurst.

IV

Jean had rented a car in London rather than go down to Pevensey by train. She had wanted to roam a little and wander freely around familiar places: through Canterbury, then on to Brede and Rye, Hurstmonceaux and Battle Abbey . . . a devious route in terms of space, but a single unit in terms of her life.

She allowed herself the luxury of two days on this short journey, then returned the car at Bexhill and finished the last seven miles of the trip by train. She installed herself in the cottage in the Old Town which she had leased for the summer and did not wait to unpack before walking out to the castle. As she had done so many times before, she wondered why she loved it so much. It had none of the grandeur of Hurstmonceaux or Bodiam and in fact reminded her irresistibly of the stump of a broken tooth. But there was always a sense of peace, a tranquil awareness of belonging to life that filled her when she came here.

She passed through the outer walls and rested briefly on their broken stones. These were the original Roman walls on which later conquerors had built. The crumbling

Norman keep, surrounded by a grass-filled ditch that had once been a moat, was ahead of her. The gently sloping ground between was occupied, not by men-at-arms, but by grazing cattle. A peaceful scene. Peaceful? She walked towards the keep and smiled. Standing by the postern gate and the steps which had once led down to the sea, Jean looked out to the new shoreline about a mile to the south across the marshes. There were far more new houses out there now than she remembered, but there were also the familiar shapes of Martello Towers, built for protection in a more recent war against Napoleon. And more recent still, she could remember the barbed wire of a modern age when what was left of an eleventh century stronghold made a magnificent machine-gun nest.

No, it was not a peaceful place—and yet it was peace she received from it.

She felt tired and turned back home. Another day she would walk out along the village, past the Mint House and the old

Courtroom, and take the road eastward across the marshes; but today she was too tired.

It was early spring. A sharp wind was blowing, but in protected spots the sun felt warm. She could taste salt on her lips and laughed for pleasure at the reminder that she had come back home.

It had been a long journey: more than thirty years of traveling through places and experiences, that had changed her appearance, her speech, and her outlook, so that she would probably be regarded as a foreigner and have to relearn her own homeland. It was doubtful that anyone would recognize or remember her now. She would simply be an eccentric stranger who took the Johnson cottage one summer and died there.

She had come home to die. She remembered herself as a young girl dreaming for hours on the cliffs of Beachy Head, watching the currents wash below, watching the wind blow through the grass, and longing to go with the wind and the waters round the world. So she had; and at heart she had always been both an explorer and an exile. She had yearned to return as passionately as she had yearned to leave.

The doctors had not understood why she refused treatment; not understood even though they had watched Tom die. It had taken Tom four years, and Jean was determined not to undergo the same. The fear and hope of diagnosis and surgeries could be faced, however terrible. They had been able to face together and accept the certainty of his death. But they had learned that it is only possible to do that once, not every day for four years. No one can live with death. They had in reality lived not with death but with deterioration, with a slowly spreading exhaustion that had eaten away at hope, at patience, at endurance, until one more treatment, one more needle were too much. To the doctors, just one more needle; but to Tom, one more effort too many. Jean did not intend to place herself in the hands of people who would fight to prolong her life when she was ready to die. She wanted strength left for the end.

She reached her cottage and stood in the doorway looking back at the castle. Life apparently had been a journey back to the beginning. The thought gave her deep satisfaction. There had been many happier lives than hers, she thought, many more exciting, but her cargo of human experience was truly her own and she was bringing it back like a ship coming home to port. She wanted to lay it to rest in this grass, to be blown by these winds, and eventually perhaps to be washed away by this sea. She could not explain to herself why. The same winds blew in the end on all and the same waters washed around the world. Logically it did not matter where she died. But in fact, it did. She was a part of this land.

HELEN OF
TROY

WHEN Menelaus saw Helen approaching him across the reddened plain of Troy, he realized that his memory had played tricks upon him. Or else time had changed her. She was far more beautiful than the woman he had known ten years before. As he watched her move towards him, years of bitterness fell away and her approaching presence made the sacrifices to regain her seem trivial. He forgot the other motives that had sustained him—the pride, the hatred, the strivings to excel—and was enveloped in something he had never known before. Dimly he remembered what one of his priests had said, that Helen was one of the crowns of life. What this meant, he did not know, but he did know that her return was not the mere recapture of an adulterous wife.

Helen herself read the eyes of Menelaus, and the eyes of the other Achaean heroes. She saw both their awareness and their lack of understanding, and she returned, silently, to be not the captive of Sparta but its glory regained. For many years afterwards she was the adornment of the bed of

Menelaus and of the festivals of his domain. Poets sang of her and wove their tales. The story in which she had played her part continued—as stories do—without her, just as it had begun without her, and yet it slowly gathered like a mist around her, as if she were the focus and the reason.

She could not be the reason for the curse upon her husband's father and his house. If Priam's family had made her the cause of their misfortunes, she could have understood, but it was the victors who centered upon her, wove their legends and their garlands of words around her, worshipped her, blamed her, enthroned her, and flaunted her as the crown of their excellence, made her their excuse, their pride, and their curse.

Menelaus died and Helen grew old. She did not grow less beautiful; she simply became beautiful in a different way. The young, lusty warriors who served her grandsons could strangely understand how a nation could go to war for ten years for such a woman. It was not the carriage of her head, nor the movement of her arms, nor the charm of her voice; but something made it easy to believe that an entire state, a league of peoples, would avenge the rape of Helen and commit any crimes necessary to regain her. She was beautiful, with a beauty beyond any dream of man's desire, and even in old age, it was clear that she had been such a prize as must not be stolen.

In the memory of men if not of poets, all this was long ago, when Helen, not too far distant from her death, attended a festival at Delphi and asked a question that had taken a lifetime to form within her. Those who knew her could not believe they heard it.

"What is it like not to suffer?"

"Before receiving the answer, you must first choose whether you wish to know it," was the reply.

Helen turned away in bewilderment and found herself looking into the face of one who was astounded by her asking such a thing. One of the few people left who re-membered events as they really had been was standing in front of her: Andromache, Hector's widow, facing her with blazing eyes and trembling with rage.

"You dare to ask about suffering! You! Desired, courted, worshipped! Thousands died because of you. A city burned for you; slavery and hunger followed you. Murder followed you. Have you known pain like mine? I watched my husband die of his wounds. I saw my home destroyed and life become an emptiness, filled only with slavery and toil and fear. Alone I have struggled to preserve my son's life—Hector's son; I have had to lie; and finally to betray the memory of my love and marry again to save my child. . . . While you have lived in luxury and ease, surrounded by the songs of poets."

Andromache's voice stopped, strangled with tears, and Helen stepped forward to enclose her in her arms. The other would have repulsed her, but was sobbing too uncontrollably and was forced to grip Helen for sheer physical support. The two aged women remained standing in an embrace, the one expressing pain and trying to hate, the other expressing love and trying to ease.

Finally Andromache, too exhausted to resist, allowed the warmth of Helen's arms to quiet her. Without protest she was placed in Helen's litter and carried to a softer bed than she had known for many years. She slept. She awoke, still weary, but in surroundings of quietness and peace, all her needs attended to, and yielding again, she slept once more.

She came to herself finally in a state of tranquillity she could not remember knowing before and looking into the eyes of Helen. Anger had deserted her, and in a kind of despair, she said, "Oh why, why are you here?"

For answer, Helen's arms moved round her with a strange, soothing tenderness that seeped into Andromache's bones. She tried to resist, but found herself too weak. Once again she wept and felt Helen's tears mingling with her own. Too weary to fight, she pleaded.

"How is it that you are not old?" said Andromache. "I am old. I can no longer see the half of what I used to see, nor hear the half. My body will no longer do what I ask; I must obey and not command it. I am tired, very tired, and for a long time now my only energy has been in hating. If you deprive me of my hatred, I shall die."

Helen's eyes widened in surprise. "But why must you hate . . . What can it give you?"

"The strength to live."

"To live for what?"

Andromache was silent. Tears slowly ran down her cheeks.

"Do you know why you live, Helen?"

"No," said Helen, and was thoughtful a long while. "Yet, in a sense I must know. At least I know that what they say is not the truth." She looked at Andromache with a sad smile. "And you know that many things have been said of me."

As the days went by Andromache seemed to weaken steadily. Death could not be far away. Helen was her constant companion, silent, but with a deep warmth and peace emanating from her that Andromache knew sustained her spirit while it sapped the forces that had maintained her body for so long.

"I think you are killing me with love," she remarked one day to Helen.

Helen smiled, "How can that be? We all die. If you are dying, love cannot be the cause; it can only ease your end."

"Then you do love me?"

"Yes."

"It is strange. I have given you no reason to love me. I thought I always hated you."

Helen again seemed surprised. "You had reason enough to hate me, I suppose. But why should I not love you? I always did, and now more than ever. You are the only person I have ever known who has accepted my love and permitted me to give it—even though you say it is costing you your life. I love you as I have never loved before, and with deep gratitude."

Andromache gazed at her in wonder. "But Paris. . . ? Your husbands. . . ?

"They desired me, but not to be loved," answered Helen. "I was a prize they wore like the ornaments on their shields or the plumes in their helmets. I truly loved Menelaus, but he refused what I had to give, and when I was young and foolish, it seemed to me that Paris sought it. I was wrong. I was wrong again when I thought ten years of war was proof that my first husband really desired my giving. I know now that war..." Her voice halted. "At times ... afterwards ... it seemed as if he was ... puzzled, perhaps."

It was Andromache now who smiled. "Puzzled? I have no doubt." Her voice changed. "Those heroes!" Suddenly she started laughing. "They fought for what? Ten years of agony and death. More than that of suffering. An excuse for Odysseus to spend twenty years away from his wife? They call you the cause of it, and you know no more than I do what they fought for. Not even Menelaus or Agamemnon knew." Her laughter became hysterical and Helen took her firmly in her arms.

"Peace, Andromache! Be calm! We suffer and we do not know why. We live and we do not know why. But it matters that we live."

"No," sobbed Andromache. "It matters that we love. That is your secret and your mystery, one that even you do not understand. No, you are not to be worn or possessed. You simply are one of the peaks of living and one that those fools never dreamed of."

Helen held her friend close until she sank again into an exhausted sleep. Watching her, she knew it would not be long before the end came. Why did it have to be now? The only time in her life that she had given love that was accepted and understood had to be with someone who was slowly, inexorably slipping away towards death. The first taste of happiness was accompanied by the greatest pain. Helen groaned in agony beside her sleeping friend.

It was not long afterwards that Andromache died, her hand in Helen's, and with a smile that tried to convey a message Helen could not read. She stood by Andromache's funeral pyre to perform the last rites of a companion and then returned to Sparta.

She had by now forgotten her question to

the Oracle and its answer. But the touch of Andromache's hand was with her for what remained of her life, giving warmth to the whole of it.